For Bella and Freddie – L.N.
For Viv and Davey – C.R.

ORCHARD BOOKS

338 Euston Road, London NW1 3BH

Orchard Books Australia

Level 17/207 Kent Street, Sydney, NSW 2000

First published in 2008 by Orchard Books

ISBN 978 1 84362 990 0

Text © Linda Newbery 2008
Illustrations © Catherine Rayner 2008

The rights of Linda Newbery to be identified as the author
and Catherine Rayner to be identified as the illustrator
of this work have been asserted by them in accordance
with the Copyright, Designs and Patents Act, 1988.

A CIP catalogue record for this book is available
from the British Library.

1 3 5 7 9 10 8 6 4 2

Printed in China

Orchard Books is a division of Hachette Children's Books,
an Hachette Livre UK company.

Posy

Linda Newbery

Catherine Rayner

ORCHARD BOOKS

Posy!

She's a . . .

. . . whiskers wiper,

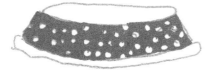

Crayon swiper.

Playful wrangler,

Knitting tangler.

Spider catcher,

Sofa scratcher.

Pillow
sitter,

Hissy
spitter!

Squabble
stirrer,

Charming
purrer.

Mirror
puzzler,

Ice cream
guzzler.

Sandwich
checker,

Board game
wrecker!

Leaf
collector,

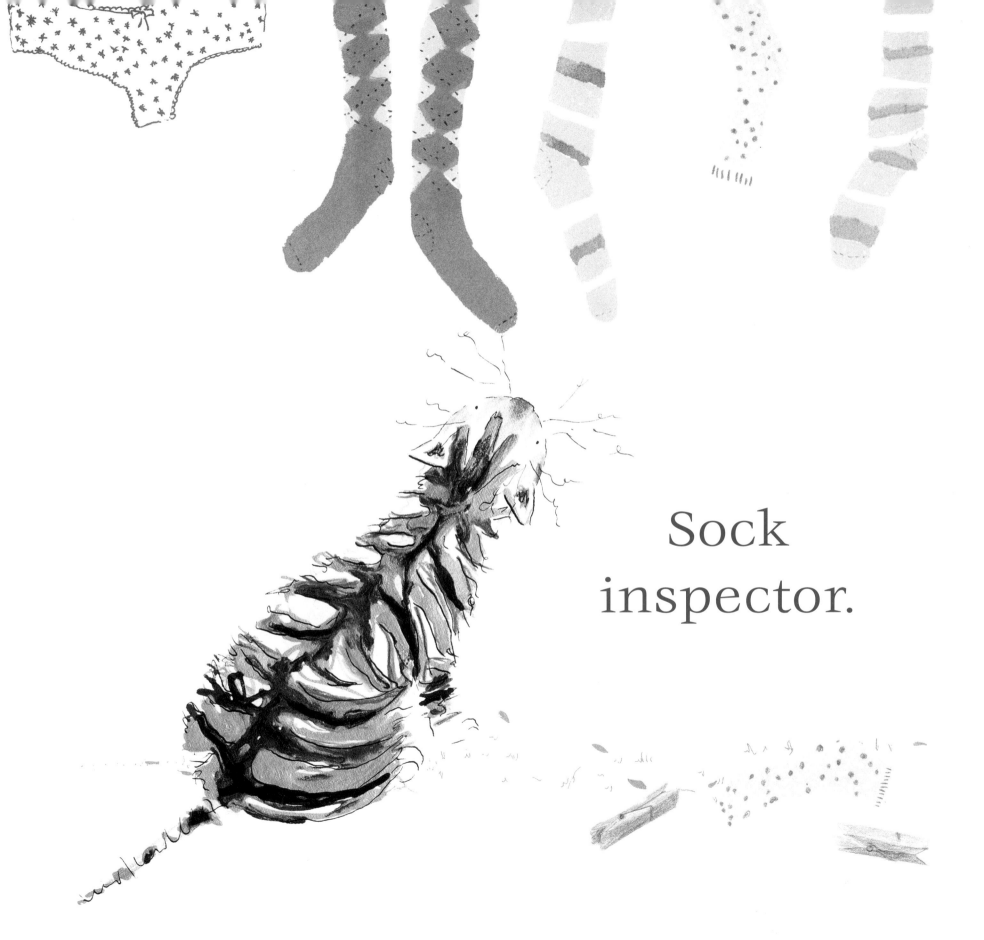

Sock
inspector.

Tomcat
fearer,

DISAPPEARER!

Dusk returner,

Cuddle
earner!

Cushion clawer,

Sprawly snorer.

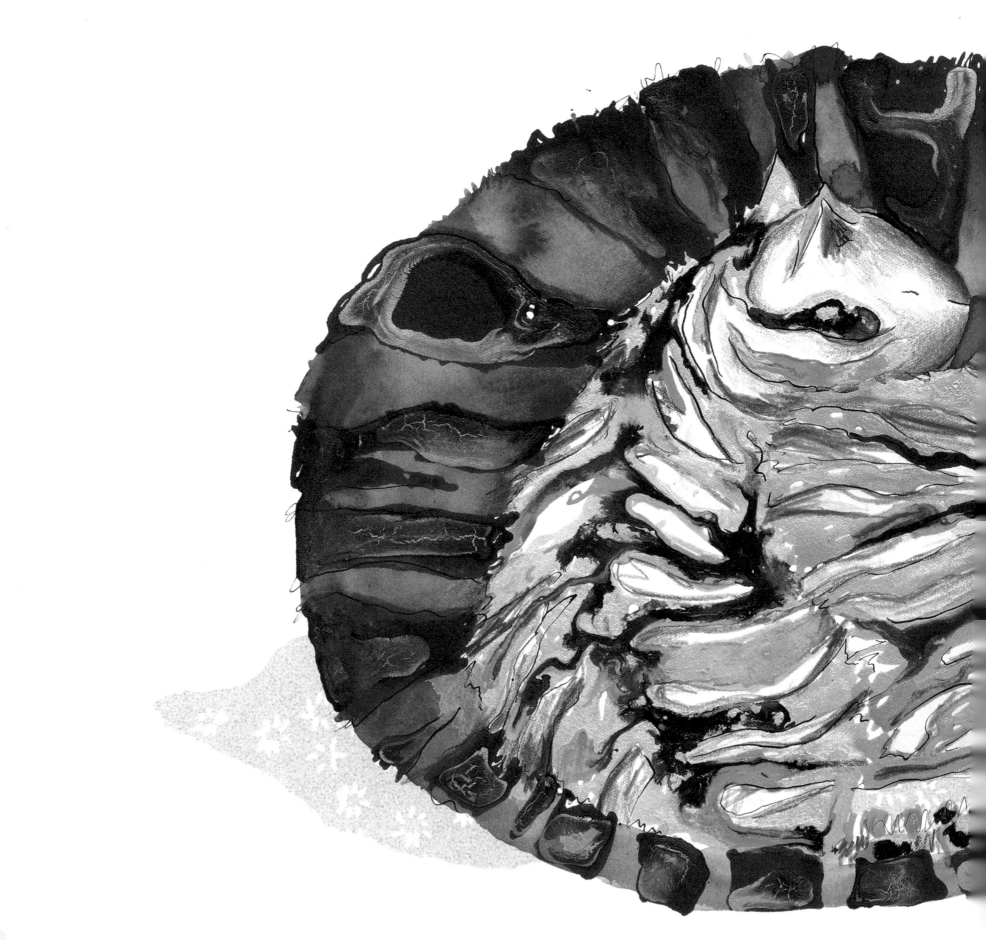

Posy!